How to Heal a Broken Wing

How to Heal a Bro

ken Wing

BOB GRAHAM

CANDLEWICK PRESS
CAMBRIDGE, MASSACHUSETTS

High above the city,

no one heard the soft thud of feathers against glass.

No one saw the bird fall.

No one looked down . . .

except Will.

Will saw a bird with a broken wing . . .

and he took it home.

A loose feather can't be put back . . .

but a broken wing can sometimes heal.

With rest . . .

and time . . .

and a little hope . . .

a bird may fly again.

Will opened his hands . . .

and with a beat of its wings,
the bird was gone.

For Lyndsay and Ella

With thanks to Rosie for her fabulous title lettering

First U.S. edition 2008

Library of Congress Cataloging-in-Publication Data

Graham, Bob, date.
How to heal a broken wing / Bob Graham. — 1st U.S. ed.
p. cm.
Summary: When Will finds a bird with a broken wing, he takes it home
and cares for it, hoping in time that it will be able to return to the sky.
ISBN 978-0-7636-3903-7
[1. Birds—Fiction. 2. Healing—Fiction.] I. Title.
PZ7.G751667Ho 2008
[E]—dc22   2007040622

2 4 6 8 10 9 7 5 3 1

Printed in Singapore

This book was typeset in Stempel Schneidler Light.
The illustrations were done in pen, watercolor, and chalk.

Candlewick Press
2067 Massachusetts Avenue
Cambridge, Massachusetts 02140

visit us at www.candlewick.com